Turkle, Brinton

Deep in the Forest

$12.95

DATE			
Te D-7	te 12A		
12/1 (M-8)			
Te 5			
te 8 mc			
2/21 (8M)			
10/12 (17)			
11/2 (15)			
te H-1			
4/23 (3)			
te 5-8			
te 1 S			
te 3			

Deep in the Forest

Deep in the Forest

by Brinton Turkle

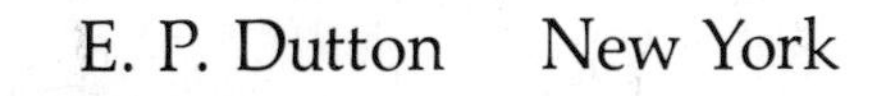

E. P. Dutton New York

Library of Congress Cataloging in Publication Data

Turkle, Brinton   Deep in the forest

SUMMARY: A curious bear explores a cabin in the forest with disastrous results.
[1. Bears—Fiction. 2. Stories without words]
I. Title.
PZ7.T847De [E] 76-21691 ISBN 0-525-28617-9

Published in the United States by
E. P. Dutton, a division of
Penguin Books USA Inc.

Editor: Ann Durell

Printed in Hong Kong by South China Printing Co.
First Edition W 10

Papa

Mama
Baby

Papa

Mama

Baby

Mama

Pa

Papa
Mama

PALEO FOR UNICORNS

AMY SUBACH

Kate Bush

PALEO FOR UNICORNS

HEALTHY COOKING FOR FEMINIST FAMILIES AND LAZY FITNESS FREAKS

AMY SUBACH

ELLY BLUE PUBLISHING
PORTLAND, OREGON

PALEO FOR UNICORNS
Healthy Cooking for Feminist Families and Lazy Fitness Freaks

ISBN 978-1-62106-208-0
Cover illustrations by Katja Gantz
Photos by Ashley Walters: cover, pages 6, 7, 13, 18, 21, 22, 34, 45, 47, 59, 63, 89, 123, 126
First edition: July 10, 2018
For a catalog or more feminist bicycle books, write or visit:
Elly Blue Publishing
2752 N Williams Ave.
Portland, OR 97227
an imprint of MicrocosmPublishing.com
Distributed by PGW and Turnaround in the UK
Printed on post-consumer paper in the USA

Library of Congress Cataloging-in-Publication Data
Names: Subach, Amy, author.
Title: Paleo for unicorns : eat the patriarchy / Amy Subach.
Description: Portland, OR : Elly Blue Publishing, [2017]
Identifiers: LCCN 2016037763 (print) | LCCN 2016035844 (ebook) | ISBN 9781621062080 (pbk.) | ISBN 9781621063469 (epdf) | ISBN 9781621062585 (epub) | ISBN 9781621061793 (mobi/kindle)
Subjects: LCSH: Quick and easy cooking. | Prehistoric peoples--Nutrition. | Physical fitness. | Child rearing. | Feminism. | LCGFT: Cookbooks.
Classification: LCC TX833.5 .S83 2017 (ebook) | LCC TX833.5 (print) | DDC 641.5/12--dc23
LC record available at https://lccn.loc.gov/2016037763

LAZER

CONTENTS

INTRODUCTION
I WANT TO KNOW, HOW DO YOU PALEO?

To win the affections of an adorable, vegan, straight-edge, college classmate, I went vegan for nine long months in 2001. During this animal-product-free gestational period, I learned a lot about cooking: for instance, that soup was something you could make yourself instead of buying it in a can. Even in hippy Portland, there weren't a lot of options for vegan food, so I learned to make my own.

Three lessons stuck with me from this episode:

- Nothing ruffles a certain type of person's feathers more than eating differently than them, which I encountered at my family's Thanksgiving that year and numerous house parties.
- Cooking well is more of a skill than an art, and with good instructions and practice you can learn to make pretty much anything.
- You shouldn't go on any type of diet to get a date.

Let me rephrase that last one: giving up cheese for nine months for some love and affection isn't worth it. However, giving up cheese because you feel much better without it is massively worth it.

In that spirit, here is a book for you. *Paleo for Unicorns* is a framework, a set of best practices, and an invitation to experiment with what works best for your health, with recipes! It is anti-authoritarian, anti-doctrinarian, anti-inflammatory, open-minded, and accepting. It's not just about the type of

food you should shove down your beautiful pie hole, it's also about feminism, exercise, parenting, and riding a bicycle!

This might be the right book for you if you have digestive issues that don't seem to go away, or a lack of energy, or need some recipes to help you manage your blood sugar, or just want to figure out a way of eating that makes you feel great.

I'm going to share my favorite paleo recipes with you. I'm going to tell you to do things like exercise, and sleep, and be nice to yourself. I'm also going to talk a little bit about approaching parenting in a more holistic and healthy way that I have coined Lazy Parenting (tm). I'm going to encourage you to change habits that make you feel bad, and adopt new habits that make you feel fantastic. You are a unicorn, and you deserve to feel fantastic.

Paleo, as I've come to define it, is a way of eating that includes meat, organ meats, vegetables (but not legumes), fruits, nuts (not peanuts because they are technically legumes), fermented foods, natural sweeteners, and sometimes dairy (raw, organic, goat, etc, if you tolerate it). It does not include grains (wheat, corn, quinoa (not really a grain actually), rice, etc), white potatoes (except sometimes it does), french fries (bummer, those are so good), processed junk foods, industrial seed oils, sugar, or alcohol. Sounds tough, I know! Luckily, there's a wonderful idea called the 80/20 rule: if you follow the paleo diet 80 percent of the time, and eat non-paleo foods 20 percent of the time, you're getting a lot of the benefits of paleo (which I talk about below), and still are able to enjoy the food and drink you want without feeling guilty. It is a way of accepting that we live in the real world and that the real world has margaritas in it.

Easy paleo (and mostly paleo) recipes make up the meat and sweet potatoes of this book. The recipes are easy, because while I love cooking and have since I was making mud biscuits in the backyard (not a euphemism for pooping outside, this time), I have two small kids and I have no patience for any recipe that is finicky, requires a lot of special ingredients, or takes a lot of time. I imagine in fifteen years I might go back to cooking like that, weighing ingredients and stuff, but for right now I'm going to leave that to other people, like professional chefs and my sweet friends who invite me over to dinner in their clean, child-free homes. Thursday nights are best for me.

One more thing: books about diet and health often make the reader feel less-than, like they need to change. Where is the desire to change coming from? Is it from feeling sick, or unhealthy? Do you want to change because you love yourself and you want yourself to be happy? I hope so! It is a perpetual challenge for me to love and accept myself in the capitalist patriarchal racist imperialist society we live in. As the badass Audre Lorde has said, "Caring for myself is not self-indulgence, it is self-preservation, and that is an act of political warfare." Please accept this book as a guideline for how you can better love and care for yourself. Let me say this: You are ALREADY worthy of love. YOU ARE A DAMN UNICORN.

PALEO IS A FAKE IDEA

So, you've probably heard about paleo and about how it's so cool and radical. You've probably also heard about how it is a FAKE IDEA. What paleo is not and cannot ever be is an accurate recreation of the way our Paleolithic Ancestors ate and lived. First of all, while we have some educated guesses, we have no way of knowing for sure what they ate. Second of all, the fruits

and vegetables and animals that are available at the grocery store or even from your local organic CSA are nothing like what people ate back then. All of that shit has been changed by human hands over the long history of time to make it easier to cultivate and way more delicious and calorically dense. Case in point: have you ever bitten into a crab apple? They are nothing at all like the Fuji or Braeburn apples we normally eat.

Our ancestors lived in very different environments with lots of different food available. They ate whatever was edible that was around them, like acorns, or whale blubber, or mangoes. Which environment is more paleo? Kind of a silly question, right? Why use the word paleo anyway? It's shorthand for saying "I don't eat grains and sugar and stuff and I eat lots of vegetables and meat and fruit and nuts."

I've been down the wormhole, the infinite world of blogs, podcasts, and books about what's "paleo" and what's not, with the experts battling about whether or not white potatoes are paleo, or is tapioca starch, or is it okay to deep fry food if you use coconut oil or lard? There are even different categories of paleo, with a whole offshoot called Primal where dairy is acceptable! And then there's low-carb paleo, and anti-inflammatory (AI) paleo, paleo for athletes, you get the idea. There are a lot of smart people who don't agree with each other about a lot of things, and it can get confusing when all you want to do is eat the "best" diet possible, or when you have digestive issues or problem skin or an auto-immune disorder and you've heard that maybe going paleo might help. It can be overwhelming to get started. My hope is that this book won't be overwhelming at all, but if it is, put it down, go for a walk, take a nap, and come back later.

Paleo is a fake idea. Unicorns are a fake idea. I love them both.

What I mean by this is that Paleo, like unicorns, doesn't really map to any one physical reality. You can, if you want, find lots of articles about how the "Paleo Diet" is made up, that our ancestors actually ate things like grains and legumes etc, that it's a fad. And you know what? I totally agree. It is made up, our ancestors ate all sorts of different shit, basically they ate what they could find that didn't kill them.

They did their best with what they had, they used knowledge passed down from their parents and grandparents and they ate what they could. Cultures, over time as they became more stable, developed all sorts of interesting food taboos and rules: feast days, prescriptions against certain foods, fasting. What we eat: it's interesting. It says a lot about where we are and who we are.

So why paleo? Why do I (loosely at times it must be said) follow and advocate for this type of eating? Honestly, mostly, because I've had good results with my health and with my family's health with it. At first, with myself at least, I was really strict about it. I was, in a word, a huge pain in the ass. (Okay that's more than one word.)

I eat dairy quite a lot. I'm off of eggs because I had a blood test say that they were NO GOOD for me. I never eat gluten, and haven't since 2008. Okay once when I was pregnant and I thought that it was okay I had a slice of pizza and regretted it.

I've been more or less eating this way since 2011, and my family has followed along with me. My husband Chris was a reluctant convert, and would eat sandwiches on regular gluten-full bread and drink beer, until one day he put two and two together and realized that beer made him feel sick. Chris is the one who convinced me and Irma, our oldest, to sell our car and live car-free. (To console Irma over the loss of our Subaru Outback, Chris bought her a

SUNDAYS
ELLIE GOULDING // HOZIER // BASSNECTAR
BRANDON FLOWERS

bright pink car that she can drive, except we stopped charging the battery because we lost the cord, so now it sits in our backyard and plays music because the radio works on a different battery.) Both of my kids think not owning a car is normal. Because it means we're going on a trip, my youngest, Isaac, thinks riding in a car seat is a real treat. He also has a bad habit of throwing rocks at cars when they drive by our house. He's got a great arm, but hasn't hit one yet, thankfully.

Sweet little unicorns, I'm here to help, and the best help I can give you is that you need to listen to your own body. Know that what works for you won't work for everybody else, and that what works for me might not work for you. Be gentle with yourself as you figure things out, and realize that things will change, and what works one week might not work the next.

There's no need to grasp and cling to a philosophy that makes you feel like crap. Try it out, and if it works, great! If it doesn't, that's okay! Take what works for you, and leave the rest. I'll still think you're magical!

WHY SHOULD I PALEO?

People try the paleo diet for many different reasons: they want to lose weight, their crossfit coach made them, they have stomach problems, skin problems, heart disease, fertility issues, auto-immune disorders, anxiety, depression, and on and on. It works for a lot of these issues, and here's my theory as to why. Okay so not really my theory, actually it's what the growing consensus in the health community is, but I'm going to go ahead and take credit here. (Hey, by the way, I am not a doctor, or a nurse, or a dietician, or anything other than a food and health geek, so please talk to a professional about this stuff, okay?)

The paleo diet largely eliminates the common sources of inflammation in the Standard American Diet (SAD: the most appropriate acronym). Chronic inflammation is probably a pretty big factor in a lot of the common diseases Americans are suffering from: specifically heart disease and diabetes, and it's looking like it plays a big role in depression and anxiety, as well as autoimmune disorders.

A little bit of inflammation is a good thing, once in a while, when there's a problem that needs to be taken care of, like a cut, or a virus. Inflammation is the body's red alert system, just like on *Star Trek: The Next Generation* when Captain Picard orders the shields raised and phasers readied. It's a stressful state that focuses the body's energies on defense. But when our bodies are constantly fighting inflammation, when we're cramming slice after slice of delicious pizza into it, when we're stressed out from driving in traffic or from work or from the constant yelling of our small children (we love them though), our bodies can't catch their breath. This is called chronic inflammation, and it's bad news. Having the shields up and being ready to fire constantly, being ready for attack at all times, is a major drain on our engines. Red alert should be for very special emergency times, not a state of perpetual worry. We want our bodies to be in a state of Rest and Digest as much as possible.

To get a bit science-y on you here, let's talk about heart disease. People with certain inflammatory markers in their blood are at higher risk for a heart attack. We hear a lot about how high cholesterol is to blame for heart disease, but the thing is, cholesterol is just doing its job, floating through your veins looking for things to repair. When it bumps into a tear—an inflamed location—it sticks to it. Then, since cholesterol sticks to itself, more and more sticks to it, and that makes a sticky clump of cholesterol which can break free and kill you, aka a blood clot. (This is an extremely oversimplified explanation

of how it works, it's all very complicated and the science is evolving but you catch my drift.)

Inflammation also begets more inflammation, so if you lower the sources of inflammation in your diet, if you exercise, if you lower your stress levels, you will have less inflammation in your veins, and you will have lowered your risk of heart disease.

We basically want our bodies to calm down, to sit in a cabin by a lake for a while and chill. One popular way paleo people do this is by doing a strict paleo diet for a limited amount of time. If you're interested in trying one of these, here are the most popular ones: the Whole 30 (whole30.com), and the 21-Day Sugar Detox Diet (21daysugardetox.com) by Diane Sanfilippo. Doing a strict paleo diet gives your body a chance to relax, to lower the red alert. Instead of thinking of this as deprivation, think of it as a vacation for your poor, overworked body.

I think these plans can be really useful! Hopefully you can approach something like this with the intention of loving yourself and taking care of yourself. Additionally, cultivate an attitude of forgiveness towards yourself if you fuck up and eat something with gluten or sugar or whatever.

If you do one of these plans, please please please slowly introduce things like gluten and dairy and sugar one at a time, maybe every three days. This way, you can observe what responses, if any, your body has to these foods. I can't tell you how many times I've heard people tell me they just went right back to pizza and ice cream the day the plan was over. And then they feel like crap and they're not sure why. You're a way smarter unicorn than that.

WORK YOUR BODY: EXERCISE

Exercise is good for you. It turns out that you don't need to do that much to benefit from it. I like exercising, sometimes. I like the things that exercising does for me more: it improves my mood, it makes me feel confident and sexy and strong, and it gives me more energy.

One of the things about extended cardiovascular exercise, like a long run or a bike ride, is that it makes you hungry. Short bursts of intense exercise don't. That's why interval training and short intense workouts (like are often done at Crossfit, or the Seven Minute Workout—there are lots of free apps and articles about this, so it's a great place to start exercising for free, and it only takes seven mintues) work really well to build muscle and lose weight. That's why you can train for an Ironman race, which can be upwards of 17 hours of cardio, and not lose any weight. There are cardiovascular benefits to both, and from my personal experience, when I got a stress echocardiogram from my cardiologist, he was very impressed with my performance and results. "You did as well as my triathletes," he said. And I never did more than twenty minutes of intense exercise at a time, three to four times a week. So you get the same benefits from shorter bursts of intense exercise as you do from extended cardio, but with the cardio you also get super hungry. Which means that if you're trying to lose weight, you'll have less success.

Lately, I've been running because it's been then best thing for my mental health, and it's simple to get out the door. My strategy has been to run until I feel better. And that usually turns out to be somewhere between 25 and thirty minutes. Well! The recent science says that you get the maximum health benefits from running from 20-30 minutes, 2 times per week! Doing more running doesn't make you healthier (though it might help to keep your weight steady as you age), and increases the risk of injury, but it can make

you a better runner, so if that's important to you, and it makes you happy, then do it!

ABOUT WEIGHT LOSS, THOUGH

If I really wanted to sell a lot of books, for the money, I'd write about how you can get rid of fat.

But, listen, I have some news for you. Women have all different kinds of bodies, and some are fat and curvy. Fat is fertile. And fertility is a good stand-in for general cis-female health. (It's not a perfect stand-in however, since there are lots of causes of infertility, and that's the kind of topic maybe a doctor should write a book about.)

We all know, intellectually, that the women's bodies we see in the media are digitally manipulated, Spanx manipulated, professional hair and make up manipulated. But knowing something only helps a bit, and I get riled up and teary when I look at magazines of ladies wearing clothes or celebrity photos. So, as a rule, I don't! You shouldn't either!

The same goes for the men among us: most of what you see as ideal is fake. Or even if it's real, the stresses that body builders go through to look good (for example, purposefully dehydrating before competition and needing IV fluids when they walk off stage) are not healthy. This is the opposite of what you want.

I don't think that "weight loss" is a good health goal. Maybe it's a goal for achieving a certain aesthetic. Maybe. Maybe if you want to spend your time obsessing about numbers it's good.

Stop obsessing about what you weigh, and start appreciating what you can do. Find a type of exercise that you enjoy, or can at least tolerate, and give yourself a while to try it out.

BICYCLING IS PALEO

Speaking of exercise, one way that I've been lucky enough to make sure I move my body every day is by going car-free, and riding a big (electric assist) cargo bike to take my kids around and get groceries in, and a smaller, regular bike when it's just me and my backpack. Sometimes I get a little sweaty, sometimes I get rained on, and I have a collection of wool gloves and rain gear and ear covers to get me through the rainy winters in Portland. It really helps that I live in a very bike-friendly city, in a very walkable neighborhood, and I'm taking advantage of it as best I can. My oldest even follows along on her bike for shorter rides. We all get to experience the seasons, and to feel elated as winter turns to spring.

While we may not know exactly what they ate, anthropologist are pretty sure that our ancestors did not sit for very long stretches of time: they walked a lot and they ran and they carried things. They probably climbed trees a bunch. If you can ride your bike instead of drive, take the opportunity to enjoy the world. The fresh air and gentle exercise will be good for your spirit. Not to mention that you will be adding less inflammatory stuff to the air that we all breathe.

There are some trade-offs we have to make as a family. We are a lot less likely to sign our kids up for far-ranging after-school activities. We stick close to home a lot of the time. But we get to really explore our neighborhood, and to

know our neighbors. We are teaching our kids the abilities and limits of their bodies.

Commuting by car is bad for us. It isolates us, it stresses us out, it raises our blood sugar and cholesterol. Cars are inflammatory. When scientists study things like how dense our bones are compared to our ancestors (denser, in this case, is better), what they find is that our modern lifestyle is robbing us of our physical health. "Sitting in a car or in front of a desk is not what we have evolved to do."

LAZY PARENTING (TM)

I was in a graduate program for therapy when I got pregnant with my first child, and boy was it difficult to sit through classes on human development when I was literally developing a human in my uterus. The terrible things we have done to baby monkeys and human children over the years unsettled me in my already unsettled pregnant state. But I learned a few key things that have put all the stress our culture puts on parents (and when we say parents we usually mean mothers, because the patriarchy), into better perspective.

First things first: yes, you are going to ruin your child(ren). Take a deep breath, accept the fact that you will do at least one thing they will always remember, and not in a good way, and forgive yourself for being exactly like every other parent in history. Even the parents that aren't there are present in their absence. As Philip Larkin wrote, "They fuck you up, your mum and dad./They may not mean to, but they do." He then goes on to tell us not to have kids at all, so, too late for me I guess.

Here's the good news: you only need to be a "good enough" parent. Most people turn out just fine. Believe me, there's a lot of research about this.

So when you make a mistake, when you lose your temper, or any of the myriad ways we are imperfect with each other, the important thing is to repair the relationship. Say you're sorry, talk about how you will do things differently next time, admit that you're imperfect. Then move on, learn from your mistakes, and don't feel guilty about it. Remember, you've already ruined them!

Modeling good repair is powerful stuff. I know my dad, for one, would never apologize for anything, even violent and destructive behavior. My mom was pretty good at the repair thing, thankfully. Being able to repair rifts in relationships is an important life skill.

I practiced Attachment Parenting pretty seriously, including co-sleeping, extended breast-feeding, and baby-wearing, mostly because a lot of it turned out to be easier. Not having to get out of bed four times a night to nurse the baby? Easier! Not having to make bottles? Easier. (Although pumping, dear lord, major props to the parents who pump. I couldn't do it.) I was, like most converts, more orthodox about it with my first kid, and by the time number two rolled around, or rather I pushed him out of my vagina, I did a better job of balancing my needs with those of my kids. There are trade-offs you make with Attachment Parenting. To talk more about breast feeding, if you're exclusively nursing, you can't really go out for very long without your baby. I missed a close friend's wedding because she didn't want any children there, and I was still nursing my daughter. I still regret it.

Kids need what we need: they want to be paid attention to, they want to be touched, they want their needs met, and they want to have fun. And they don't want their parents to be stressed out all the time, promise me.

NEW SEASONS

Most importantly, put your own mask on first. Get a babysitter, or ask a friend to watch your kid, and go on a date, and it doesn't have to be with anyone but yourself. Join a gym that has childcare and put the baby in childcare for 45 minutes and sit in the sauna or do some gentle stretching or watch reality TV while gently circling your feet around the elliptical. My sister-in-law and her husband would drop their son off at the gym daycare and sit on the couch in the gym and talk to each other. Do whatever you can to remind yourself every damn day that you're an amazing unicorn who isn't just a milk machine or a bottle warmer.

Specifically for parents who breastfeed, your body will deplete itself to feed your child. Eat. It is stupid to restrict calories while pregnant or breastfeeding. Focus on eating lots of healthy foods, sure. Many traditional cultures encourage pregnant (or newly married) women to eat foods that are high in Omega-3 fatty acids, like sardines. And drink water.

And relax. Parenting is stressful, stress causes inflammation, and remember what we said about that? Take care of yourself so you can watch little baby graduate from clown college.

JACKSON'S
HONEST
COCONUT OIL
POTATO CHIPS

HOW TO EAT PALEO

OKAY, COOL, BUT WHAT SHOULD I EAT? OR MEAL PLANNING

I'll admit I'm not super great at planning meals in advance. Sorry, I'm not much of a planner and you can find a 30 day paleo meal plan on the internet pretty easily. But I do have a basic framework for most of my meals, and it looks like this.

Breakfast: my kids get banana pancakes or eggs and sauerkraut and yogurt and maybe a smoothie. Which is what I used to eat until I found out I have an egg allergy. Now I eat a smoothie with frozen kale and berries and a half a banana and protein powder (when you think about it, the whole concept of protein powder isn't paleo, but I've seen paleo experts recommend different sources of protein powder, including pea and egg, so shrug?) and some sort of liquid, yogurt or almond milk or goat kefir. Occasionally I'll make a batch of paleo porridge (NOatmeal) for the kids.

Lunch: Honestly, more often than I'd like to admit, tacos. Ideally, a salad with leftover meat and vegetables. Or just leftovers cold from the fridge.

Dinner: Cooked vegetable, meat, sweet potato, salad.

It's so repetitive, but I'm pretty happy with it. My motto is KISSU: Keep It Simple, Shiny Unicorns! You'll find recipes for all of it below.

FAMILY MEAL PLANNING: FEED THE CHILDREN LUNCH

I must've been in 3rd grade or so when Lunchables became a thing. I remember seeing the commercials and asking my mom for them in the grocery store and her agreeing. I also remember how disgusting they were.

I remember eating a cold, not toasted, gummy bagel and cream cheese from a packet and a can of Hawaiian Punch for lunch in 8th grade. This was in New York, ostensibly the bagel capital of America.

How did they get away with serving us such junk?

Now I have a child who eats lunch at preschool five days a week, and it's a lot of responsibility. You know what she usually gets? Leftovers, an apple, a cheese stick, some carrot sticks or other chopped vegetables, and maybe some sweet potato cubes. Occasionally she gets salami and olives. Nothing fancy or elaborate. In the summer she gets watermelon or berries too. And she usually eats most of it.

I pack lunch when I'm cleaning up after dinner so that I don't have to think about it in the morning. Usually when I'm cooking dinner I put aside her lunch before I serve us dinner, to be sure there's enough.

When there's nothing left over, I'll hard boil a couple of eggs for her. She really likes them.

Sometimes she eats everything. Sometimes she eats part of it. I try not to fuss about it too much because I don't think it's good to make kids feel anxious about what they eat. If you put healthy food in front of them 90% of the time, and if they see you eating healthy food, they will eat what they need. (Usually. There are of course various medical exceptions to this.)

We do have one policy around meal times: the No Thank You Bite. You have to take one bite of the new/disliked food (and swallow it). Sometimes the No Thank You Bite turns into a Yes, Please Bite and that's a parenting win!

As for the rest of the time, offer your kids the same stuff you're eating, cut up and cooled off as necessary. This will of course be easier when they are babies, before they get all opinionated and willful.

LE SHOPPING

When I first made the transition to paleo, a lot of the ingredients were harder to find, things like coconut flour, almond flour, lard, grass fed beef. Now, there's paleo protein bars, paleo cake mixes, paleo breakfast cereals, paleo potato chips. It's become quite the marketing buzzword. And I think that a lot of these convenience paleo foods are fine, but they're very expensive, and mostly incredibly simple to make at home.

There's lots of ways to economize and eat paleo style: farmers markets and CSAs, buy a half of a cow or pig and freeze it, even Costco has a lot of good deals on coconut oil etc.

For most recipes, the most exotic thing you'll need is nice coconut oil or lard. The desserts require ingredients that are outside of the standard American pantry, and I think this is okay, because dessert should be special.

I use a lot of almond flour in my baking, but there's an almond shortage, and almonds have gotten really expensive. Since I don't bake very frequently anymore, this hasn't been much of an issue for me, but I'm starting to make the shift to other nuts and nut flours. It's good to change things up! Hazelnuts are native to the Pacific Northwest, where I live, so I've been adding those in

CELEBRATE
GOOD FOOD

NEW SEASONS MARKET
SLICED ORGANIC
CRIMINI MUSHROOMS
$4.99
NET WT
6 oz

to the rotation more. They are a less neutral tasting nut, though, so the results are noticeably different.

SUPPLIES

I've been cooking and baking for a long time, and I've purchased many things I did not need and did not use. It's embarrassing. And then there's all the stuff I love but don't use any more, post-gluten.

Don't make my mistakes. Here's what you need. (I'm not going to list things like plates and silverware, you know you need those right I hope?)

Immersion blender/stick blender/regular blender. An immersion blender is a stick shaped blending device that you, um, stick into the stuff you want to blend. They're more suited for softer materials—I've broken two immersion blenders making smoothies. Those frozen strawberries are tough. I'm on my third one. I use mine multiple times a day to make pancakes, smoothies, soups, frosting, cake, etc. You can make awesome mayonnaise/aioli with these as well. You cannot make your own nut butter with one, though, and it's not really a replacement for a food processor. I use a regular blender and an immersion blender every day.

Cast iron skillets. Heavy, oven- and fire-proof (I take mine camping), and great at retaining heat, cast iron skillets are old-fashioned and indispensable. I have four now, from tiny to humongous. I bought them all used, and they are of varying quality, and did I mention they are heavy, but they are work horses and can take whatever you throw at them. There's lots of info about cleaning and seasoning them out there. I treat mine pretty rough but they have held up just fine! A well tended cast iron pan is way better than a non-

stick skillet, as it is almost as non-sticky, you're not going to ruin it if you accidentally use a metal utensil, and it won't leech non-stick compounds into your food.

Instant-read digital thermometer. It is so much easier to cook meat with one of these. There is no guessing. There are lots of ways to tell if meat is cooked, but none as accurate as a thermometer. I have a great digital one from Sur La Table and it was $15 and I get very upset when it's missing or the battery dies. You can replace the battery! Also great to have is an analog thermometer, the kind you can stick in a roast and leave in the oven.

Slow cooker/crock pot. You can use this to make stock, to cook meat, to make soup, to keep your mulled wine warm all winter long. Counter-intuitively, this is a great way to cook during the hot summer months as it won't heat up your house as much as an oven will. Also, you can't go to a thrift store without seeing one for sale. They make fancy digital programmable ones nowadays too. When mine breaks I might get a fancy one with a timer!

Large mixing bowls. Use them for making cookies, or serving salad. I have two really big bowls, but only ever need one except on Thanksgiving, when I need four.

Large stock pot. For making soup, if you don't have a slow-cooker.

Baking sheets/sheet pans. Useful for everything from roasting vegetables to baking cookies to freezing berries. Get two of these.

Thin metal spatula. For egg frying, cookie lifting, and banana pancake flipping. Mine is by OXO and I buy a new one every two years because it breaks.

Silicon spatula. For batter and mayonnaise scraping.

Parchment paper. For baking cakes, cookies, anything sticky. Also good for freezing bananas and fruit.

NICE, BUT NOT NECESSARY:

Food processor. Not as important as the immersion blender, but if you want to make nut butter/flour, or if you hate chopping vegetables, it's worth it. Or at least worth asking for.

Julienne vegetable peeler. This is like a regular vegetable peeler, except that it makes tiny little noodles out of your vegetables. For making zucchini noodles, fancy carrot salads, impressing guests.

Cookie scooper. This is a melon baller type gadget that has a special piece of metal that, when you squeeze the handle, releases whatever you've scooped up. Great for filling mini muffin pans, or scooping tiny ice cream scoops, or sticky cookie dough dispensing. If you're particular about consistently sized cookies, you're going to love this.

Mini muffin tins. Since smaller things cook faster and I'm impatient.

RECIPES

BREAKFAST BREAKDOWNS

It used to be that the gospel of breakfast was that you had to eat it. Studies were done that showed that people who ate breakfast weighed less, had more brain power thoughts, and could lift small cars over their heads. And then, some other people were like, actually, no, not exactly true. Science!

I eat breakfast because I have to, I cannot even wait until ten in the morning to eat or I start to get shaky and sweaty, and mean. This is why if I go out to brunch, I eat breakfast first. You might be different! Kids, though, they probably need to eat breakfast.

Some people intentionally fast until lunch, or just have a butter/coconut oil coffee (recently popularized by a fad diet, but the idea of mixing fat into your hot morning breakfast beverage goes all the way back to drinking yak butter tea).

When I lived in Japan one summer in high school, my homestay family made the best breakfasts: miso soup, leftover dinner, small salad. Except, since my homestay mother, Midori, was so caring and thoughtful and wanted me to feel at home, she made me french bread pizza with sliced up hot dogs. It was gross. Sweet, thoughtful, and gross.

Emulating the traditional Japanese style of breakfast, leftovers, is actually a pretty great way to do it. Westerners are so wrapped up in the whole idea of breakfast as a sugary, sweet, special meal. Even in France a typical breakfast is bread and nutella, or a croissant, with hot chocolate for the kids and coffee

for the grown ups. Think about what most people eat for breakfast: cold cereal and milk, pop tarts, bagel and cream cheese.

Eating protein and some fat and some carbs for breakfast is a good idea. I find that I function pretty well mentally and physically if I have carbs in the morning. There was a time when I ate three eggs and sauerkraut every morning, but I'd always get hungry and feel mentally foggy in a couple of hours. When I switched to kale smoothies, I noticed I had more energy.

Try an experiment for a couple of weeks. Do a more protein and fat heavy breakfast for a week, like eggs, bacon, sauerkraut, and see how you feel. Then try a breakfast with more carbs for a week, like a fruit and kale smoothie with protein powder and nut butter, or Banana Pancakes. You might feel better with one or the other.

HARD BOILED EGGS

Take your eggs out of the fridge and put them in a small pot. Cover them with one inch of water. Put the pot on the stove over high heat until it comes to a boil. Take the pot off of the heat, cover with a lid, and let sit for ten to twelve minutes. Less time for softer yolks. Rinse the eggs under cool running water and eat, or put in the fridge for a quick breakfast or afternoon snack.

Bonus hint: decorate the hard boiled eggs with sharpie or another marker so that you can tell the difference between them and the raw eggs. Suggestions: "You're eggsactly what I needed." "Have an eggcellent day!" "You crack me up."

BACON

It's faster to cook bacon in a pan on the stove, but it's cleaner and less risky to cook it in the oven. You don't need to pay as much attention, and the results are more consistent.

Line a rimmed baking sheet with aluminum foil, or grab a nice big cast iron skillet. Turn the oven on to 300 degrees F. Spread out some bacon in the pan or sheet, trying not to overlap too much. Put the bacon in the oven for about 30 minutes. You don't need to stir it, just keep an eye on it. It won't burn quickly at this temperature, and I like my bacon super crispy.

If you're in a rush, you can turn the oven up as high as 350 degrees. But you'll need to pay attention.

BUTTER COFFEE

Sometimes, I love butter coffee. Sometimes it grosses me out. Here's how I do it.

Make coffee. Put it in a blender with about a teaspoon to a tablespoon of butter or coconut oil or a mix. Blend it until it is frothy, and drink it while it's hot. When it cools down the fat hardens on the top and it's not emulsified and creamy, but I'm not above drinking it.

I went to this food cart in Austin, Texas that made coffee like this, and they also made this delicious mocha thing, with cocoa powder and maple syrup and butter and it was $8 for 16 ounces and I totally went back for another one the next day, even though it was a rip off. It was so good. You could try making something like that too, but I haven't.

SMOOTHIES

I make myself one kind of smoothie every morning, and here is what is in it.

Half a banana

Frozen Kale/Spinach (half a cup? I don't measure)

Frozen blueberries or strawberries or whatever we have (same amount as the kale)

Whey or other protein powder you like

Yogurt (full fat dairy if you tolerate it, alternative if you don't)/goat kefir/nut milk

Water

Sometimes a scoop of nut butter

APPLE PIE EGGS

The original recipe I saw for these was called "Paleo French Toast." I can kind of see how these are like french toast. But if you served them to someone expecting french toast, you might not get another chance to serve them breakfast.

What this is is a recipe for cooked apple slices and eggs. It's great! Irma is completely into it. I made it this morning and she asked to take some of it off of her dad's plate. It's also appropriate if you're doing the 30-Day Sugar Detox, if you use green apples only.

Apples vary in size a lot. I think a good ratio is one fist-sized apple (not huge, not tiny) to three eggs. You'll have to use your judgement and adapt to your taste. The recipe below serves 2 hungry adults, or two moderately hungry adults and really hungry preschooler.

3 apples

1 tablespoon butter or coconut oil

7-8 eggs

1-2 teaspoons vanilla

2 teaspoons cinnamon

pinch salt

Thinly slice three medium sized apples (this morning I used one huge Granny Smith and one medium Cameo). Making the slices smaller is a great idea too, as they are easier to stir and eat.

In a cast iron skillet (6-8 inches, with a high rim), add one tablespoon of butter, the sliced apples, a sprinkle of cinnamon, and stir. Cook until softened.

In a medium bowl, crack 7-8 eggs. Add a teaspoon or two of vanilla, cinnamon, and a pinch of salt and whisk until blended.

Now, here's the choose your own adventure part. You can either add the eggs to the apples on the stove and carefully stir until the eggs are cooked, or you can add the eggs and put the pan in the oven at 350 degrees Fahrenheit, and wait until the eggs are puffed up. Stove top option is much faster and more like an apple pie scramble. Oven option takes longer (depending on the size of your pan and whether or not you've preheated the oven), and is more of a fritatta.

You could also throw some frozen blueberries in with the apples, that'd be pretty yummy.

BANANA PANCAKES

Pancakes were my least favorite breakfast food, back in the gluten days. They were usually from a mix, and usually heavy and made me feel gross. Syrup ruled, so I tolerated them as a vehicle for syrup.

Banana pancakes, however, need no syrup of any kind. In fact, they are great dipped in plain whole milk yogurt. Here's the base recipe for one person.

1 banana

3 eggs (2 works also, especially if it's a smaller banana)

½ tsp cinnamon

splash vanilla extract

pinch salt (Optional, especially if you use salted butter)

butter or oil for cooking

Blend all ingredients except for the butter. Pour silver dollar sized pancakes onto a medium hot buttered griddle until they brown around the edges and look solid (not shiny), then flip (this is where you'll wish you had a thin metal spatula). These cook fairly quickly, but the pancakes need to be fairly small. Smaller than a saucer or else they won't flip nicely. Serve with yogurt or honey or whatever. Use them as taco shells and fill them with bacon.

Variations

Add a tablespoon of nut butter

Use two eggs for a denser pancake

- Double the recipe, but instead of two bananas, use one banana and one half cup of cooked sweet potato or pumpkin puree
- Add some whole nuts before you blend for crunch
- Add mini chocolate chips
- Add blueberries
- Add shredded coconut

NOATMEAL, OR PALEO PORRIDGE

Make this porridge, and you can pretend you're one of the three bears and chase your kid around the house yelling "Who has been eating my porridge?"

2 bananas

2 cups of mixed nuts (unsalted please)

3 eggs

1 tablespoon vanilla extract

2 teaspoons cinnamon or pumpkin pie spice

Optional nut milk or water to thin the batter

Butter or oil for cooking

In a blender of some sort, put two bananas, two cups of nuts (almonds and cashews work great, an assortment is best), and three eggs, a tablespoon of vanilla, and two teaspoons of cinnamon. Blend these up until they are quite smooth, but really you can make this with almost any texture and it'll be yummy. If you want, if the batter seems too thick, blend in some water or nut milk.

Put some fat in a small sauce pan, on medium low heat. When it is melted, add the sloshy nut mixture, and cook, stirring frequently, until it thickens up and is hot all the way through. Serve with maple syrup or berries. Leftovers are great eaten cold

MEATY MAINS AND SALTY SEAFOODS

When you're a paleo unicorn, you're going to get a lot of your calories/energy from meat, though vegetables should take up about 75% of your plate. So please, buy the best meat you can afford, when you can. And I don't mean the most expensive cuts, I mean the grass fed local organic kind, where the pigs get mud massages on the way to the local abattoir. You can look for a local farm that sells half cows, or find a farmer's market with a good meat purveyor and find other ways to make eating quality meat more affordable.

Also, try to eat a variety of meat and seafood. Lamb is underrated, and you can mix some ground lamb in with your regular hamburger meat and it's extra yummy but not overpowering in its lamb-ness.

SLOW COOKER MEAT

I used to try really hard to make roasts in the oven. And sometimes, following a recipe, with the moon waxing, and all of my ingredients in order, I succeeded.

Which is to say I usually failed. And then I tried a slow cooker.

You can succeed too. I believe in you and your slow cooker.

Go and buy a roast. I usually buy a pork shoulder or something. 3-4 pounds seems to work best. It can have a bone in it. Ask your butcher, if you have one. Say to her, "I'm looking for a piece of meat to throw in my slow cooker and ignore all day and then eat that will be amazing." She will tell you what to buy.

Go home. In the morning, wake up, drink coffee, consider showering, eat breakfast, and then get out your slow cooker. Turn it on low. Take your hunk of meat out of the fridge. Sprinkle and rub salt and pepper all over it. Put it in the slow cooker. Cover. Come back in six to eight hours, shred the meat with a fork and mix it up with the juices in there, and eat it. Try not to eat all three pounds of meat at once because you will want leftovers.

Now, if you're feeling fancy, you can always add dried oregano, or a cup of apple cider (hard or not), or a jar of tomato puree, or some whole garlic cloves, or a bunch of chopped carrots and other root vegetables. But you really don't need to add anything. My god, you could even brown the meat before putting it in the slow cooker. But I feel like that just makes a big mess and doesn't add much, maybe a little extra crispiness. YOLO.

APPLE CIDER PORK SHOULDER

Get a pork shoulder, maybe 2-3 pounds. Salt and pepper it. Brown it on all sides (or don't!). Put it in a slow cooker with a bottle of hard apple cider and some cut up apples and some onion if you feel like it, and maybe even sprinkle some cinnamon on it. Let it cook on low for 8 hours. This is great with Marinated Kale Salad (on page 97).

Carnitas

Pork shoulder roast, boneless, 2-3.5 pounds

Salt

Serve with:

Cilantro, washed and chopped

Small white onion, diced

Whole leaf lettuce, like romaine hearts

Avocado

CARNITAS

Get a 2-3 pound pork shoulder, trim the excess fat (but leave some), and cut it up into 2 inch cubes. Salt it, and put it in the slow cooker with about a cup of water, on low, with the lid slightly askew so that the steam can evaporate. Cook for six hours, until the water is gone, stirring very infrequently. Transfer to a heavy bottomed pot, turn the heat up to medium, and cook for another 1-2 hours, so that the fat from the shoulder starts to render and fry the pork. You have to stick around and pay attention to this. When it's crispy and salty and good, serve it on lettuce wraps with cilantro and onions and hot sauce or avocado.

CHICKEN FOR DAYS

I believe in not having to think about things too much.

I believe that if you buy a (pasture raised, antibiotic-free, happy etc) whole chicken and bring it home, there should not be a question in your mind about what you are supposed to do with it. Of course there are options and variations and improvisations available, but what you need, what we all need, is a simple game plan that will work. I'm going to give you two simple game plans for that chicken, which is probably somewhere between the size of a football and soccer ball, so a game plan is what you need. Interestingly enough, both game plans turn into soup. Like our fleshy bodies one day will also turn into soup in the ground. Um, but different? Because, like, don't serve corpse soup at a dinner party, unless it's Halloween or maybe the Zombie Apocalypse and you want, nay, need to fit in. Then, serve corpse soup.

So you got a chicken. Unwrap it. Remove whatever might be inside it. Sometimes I use the organs for stock, but usually I give them to my dog as part of his dinner. Rinse the chicken with cold water. (This is optional, and *Consumer Reports* says you shouldn't do this because it sprays salmonella all over your sink, which is a good point, but I do it anyway.)

GAME PLAN A: CHICKEN SOUP

Whole chicken

5 garlic cloves (more or less)

3 ribs celery

3-4 carrots

1 sweet potato, peeled and diced

olive oil or coconut oil

Around two tablespoons total of a variety of fresh or dried herbs, like thyme, bay leaf, rosemary, oregano, star anise.

Salt and Pepper to taste

Chop up some carrots, celery, an onion (any color will do), maybe some sweet potatoes, a couple cloves or up to a full head of garlic.

In a large stock pot on medium-high heat, add some oil of your choice, then add the vegetables—but NOT THE GARLIC. Stir a bit so they don't burn, and watch them as the start to soften. This will take maybe five minutes? Maybe ten? When the veg are soft, add the garlic, and stir for another minute.

(Why don't we just add the garlic right away? Because garlic is a picky snot and will burn on you in the blink of an eye, and ruin everything.)

Now, put the whole chicken in the pot, and add filtered water to cover, and put back on the stove until it boils.

You can add some fresh or dried herbs at this point. Thyme, bay leaf, rosemary, oregano, star anise, mix it up!

Then turn down the heat and cook until the chicken is cooked. You can leave it in there longer, it will not dry out too bad, but if you take it out before it's cooked you'll be all grossed out in the next step.

How can you tell if the chicken is cooked? You can either use a meat thermometer, which is kind of tricky in a soup situation, what with all the boiling liquid, or you can do the joint test. If the thigh bone wiggles easily, your chicken is cooked.

Now, be careful, use tongs, use long sleeves and oven mitts, and slowly remove the chicken from the pot and place it on a large cutting board with a moat for the juices, or put it in a roasting pan. Let it cool down. Turn the heat on the soup down to low, taste the broth, add salt and pepper or anything else that tickles your fancy, wash some dishes, pet the dog, whatever you need to do to keep yourself occupied while the chicken gets a chance to rest.

Now, chop up the chicken, and put it back in the pot. Not the bones, probably not the skin, but the meat. Bones can go in the compost, skin can go to the dog.

You can also add some chopped up greens if you feel like it. Life is short and don't forget about the heat death of the universe.

GAME PLAN B: PART 1: ROAST CHICKEN

Whole chicken

1 tablespoon Salt

1-2 teaspoons Garlic powder

Optional: lemon

For absolute best results, take your chicken, put it in a bowl, cover it with salt and garlic powder, and put it in the fridge for the day, or at least an hour. This will dry out the skin and make it super crispy. If you didn't think ahead (which is usually the case for me), you can salt the chicken while the oven is heating up. Additional seasoning options: tbsp thyme or rosemary or oregano, squeeze of lemon.

Put a large cast iron skillet in the oven, and preheat to 450 F.

Put on your butcher hat. There is skin connecting the breast of the bird to the thigh/drumstick. Use scissors or a sharp paring knife to cut a line in that skin. Now dislocate the thigh bone from the pelvis/back bone on both sides by pulling the thigh away from the breast until you hear a pop. You can skip this part if you want. Sometimes I do. But I enjoy it. I understand you might not.

Now, if your oven is hot and your skillet is ready, carefully, because this part is splashy and sizzly, place the chicken in the pan, thigh-side down. Let it cook for about 45 minutes to an hour, until the meat thermometer says the breast meat is 165-170 degrees F. I err on the 170 side because I like to really know my meat is cooked. Take out the pan, let the chicken rest for five minutes while you scramble to get everything else ready, then carve up and serve.

More options: put some carrots or cauliflower or onions in with the chicken. They'll probably burn if you put them in at the same time, but if you wait like 15 minutes or so they won't burn. They will get all the yummy chicken fat all over them.

★ ★ ★ ★ ★ ★ ★ ★ ★ ★

PART 2: CHICKEN STOCK

Cooked chicken carcass and bones

1 tablespoon Apple Cider Vinegar

Optional: leftover celery leaves, carrot tops, garlic head, peppercorns (whole), bay leaf.

Take the carcass, including any not too crispy skin, and the wings and bones from the thighs, put it into a slow cooker with filtered water and a tablespoon (I never measure) of Apple Cider Vinegar, and cook it on low for a day. Two days, if you add more water. This will get more of the minerals and stuff out of the bones.

Optional and extra yummy: add some chopped celery leaves, stalks, carrot tops, garlic heads, onion halves, one or two hours before you strain it. Also a bay leaf is a good thing, and peppercorns. I'm always out of bay leaves.

Strain into a bowl. (This is the part where I end up covered in chicken broth and cursing, so use caution.)

Freeze, or use for Part 3: Soup of the Day.

Chicken stock

Onion, red or white or yellow, any kind

3 -4 carrots

1-2 Celery ribs

Any other vegetables you like! Seriously!

Spices

Salt and Pepper

I feel ridiculous writing this down. It's so simple. It takes a lot of work, but it's so simple.

Chop up an onion, three carrots, a rib of celery, and add to a medium high stock pot with oil/butter. Cook and stir until soft.

Add other vegetables. Zucchini, or butternut squash. An apple or two is incredibly yummy and sweet in soup. Or some sweet potatoes. Add as much garlic as you can handle. Add some spices.

Add the Broth. Bring to a simmer. Cook until the vegetables are cooked.

Option: blend your soup, adding cream or something like that. Or eat it chunky.

Option: Put raw spinach in a bowl and pour the hot soup over it.

Option: Top with some chevre.

SWEET AND SIMPLE SOUP

This is a blended, creamy soup that I love.

1 tbsp olive oil or butter

1 -2 tsp chopped fresh ginger

1 medium red apple, chopped, skin on

1 large yam

3-4 carrots, sliced into circles

4-6 cups chicken stock, hot

1 tbsp cinnamon

½ tsp cardomom

Pinch of freshly grated nutmeg

Salt and pepper to taste

In a large pot with a lid, melt the butter/oil over medium heat. Add the ginger, apple, yam, and carrots and stir for a few minutes until the ginger is fragrant. Add the hot chicken stock and the spices, and stir to combine. Bring to a boil, turn down the heat to low and simmer covered until the vegetables are soft. Blend with an immersion blender, or in batches in a regular blender. Taste, and add salt if necessary.

1/2-2/3 pounds of Clams per person

1-2 tablespoons Butter or coconut oil

3 cloves (or more!) Garlic

1 bunch flat leafed Parsley

White wine or apple cider for cooking

Lemon

Kids love clams because they are cool! You can clean the shells when you're done by boiling them and then make art projects.

Buy some clams, a half-pound per person, because truth be told you're mostly buying shells. Manila clams are great. Take them home and scrub the sand away in cold water. Keep cold, but make sure they can breath, as in, don't wrap them up tight in a plastic bag.

Chop up one-two garlic cloves per pound of clams.

Chop up some flat leafed parsley.

Put a good amount of butter or ghee into a big pot that has a lid. Melt it on high heat, add the chopped garlic, and cook until fragrant. (One minute at most)

Add the clams and stir.

Add liquid to a depth of one to two inches. I love using chicken broth or white wine or both, but water is acceptable too.

Cover the pot and steam the clams. This takes very little time. You'll know they are cooked when they have all opened up.

Remove from heat. Squeeze a lemon over them, top with parsley. Serve with something to soak up the broth. The garlicky broth is amazing. Sweet potatoes are great for this.

CRISPY SKIN SALMON

Skin-on salmon filet (go for wild line caught if you can)

Butter

Salt and Pepper

Lemon

Dill (optional)

Describing something as "Crispy Skin" gives me the creeps a little bit. Anyway, I go through phases when I hate the idea of cooking fish at home because if you don't clean the pan up right away the whole house smells like fish and that bugs me. But I have a great way to cook salmon, or any fatty fish with skin attached. The skin is really nutritious, and this method makes it almost like bacon. Fishy bacon.

You can use any thickness fish for this method. But, if you're using a really thin filet, consider skipping the oven part and just cooking it on the stove.

Preheat your oven to 425.

Generously salt, pepper, and spice the salmon filet on both sides. Dill is a traditional standard go-to for this.

Heat up a cast iron skillet that's large enough for the fish over medium-high heat. The pan should be fairly hot. Add butter to the pan and place the salmon skin side up in the hot butter. Cook for a few minutes, until you can see the salmon beginning to brown. Carefully flip the fish skin side down, and put pan in the hot oven. Feel free to blob some butter or some other fat on top of the fish so it doesn't dry out so much.

Here's where you get to choose. I like my cooked fish cooked all the way, well done. I wait until the salmon starts weeping its white protein tears, that way I know the skin will be crispy too. If you want your fish a little rare—like a fancy pants—take it out sooner. I'll just eat the more cooked parts on the end.

Serve, making sure to scrape the crispy skin off the pan, with lemon wedges.

GRAIN-FREE MAC & CHEESE

This is a sort of complicated one-skillet leftover-utilizing meal, in that you need to make the cauliflower and/or cabbage before. If you plan ahead and have cauliflower and cabbage for dinner the night before, and you just don't eat all of it in one sitting, then it's a brilliant use of leftovers. Sometimes you remember and sometimes you don't. Don't beat yourself up.

Head of Cauliflower and/or Cabbage

Butter or oil

Onion

1 teaspoon paprika

1 teaspoon ground caraway

4 eggs

1 cup heavy whipping cream

1 teaspoon paprika

1 teaspoon ground caraway

1.5 cups grated cheese: Parmesan, Swiss, Gruyere

Onion, diced

2 cups sliced brown mushrooms

1 teaspoon paprika

1 teaspoon ground caraway

Package of Canadian or regular bacon (optional)

It starts with an onion.

Okay no it starts with cooking a head of cauliflower in a pot with some water until it's cooked, and/or roasting some cabbage or cauliflower in the oven at 400 degrees F with some olive oil and paprika and ground caraway and salt and pepper. Roast the cauliflower/cabbage until it's browned. And eat some of both with a steak or something. But don't eat all of it! Then put the leftovers in the fridge and go to sleep and have sweet dreams about overthrowing the kyriarchy.

Sleep well? Great! You're still going to have to wait because this would be a strange breakfast, but what do I know?

Preheat oven to 350 degrees F.

Remove four hippy local pastured eggs and some hippy local heavy whipping cream from your fridge, about a cup of cream, maybe more. Crack eggs and pour cream in the same bowl. Add paprika and caraway and salt and pepper. Whisk it. Into shape. Then add a cup of grated parmesan cheese and a smidge of other cheeses you might have around the house because your Mother-in-Law was visiting and cheese is delicious. I used a bit of Swiss Emmentaler. I didn't grate it, I cut it up kind of small though. Waste not want not.

Now, the onion. Cut up one large onion and cook it with some fat (I used olive oil) in your big cast iron skillet until it's translucent-plus. Then add two cups of sliced brown mushrooms, paprika, caraway, salt and pepper to taste. I don't know how much. A sprinkling. Use your common sense. Cook this until the mushrooms are nice and soft and cooked. Remove to a plate.

Vegetarian? Skip this part. Cut up some Canadian bacon (do I need to tell you to get the best kind of pig-life bacon you can buy? I don't, you know better), and sautee it in the skillet until browned a bit. You could also use regular bacon but I didn't and I think it would be a different kind of thing but that's cool. Dude, you could use tofu, just keep it away from my face okay? (Said the former vegan.)

Add the mushroom-onion mix back.

Chop up the cold cauliflower and cabbage. Make it small. Add to skillet. Stir.

Turn off the heat. Pour the egg cream cheese mix on top of the other stuff and smoosh it all down. Put in the oven until it puffs up and is not jiggly. Eat all of it. It's really good cold too if you can control yourself. This amount served the three of us pretty well with a big green salad on the side.

Listen, you could definitely add more cheese to this. I'm not going to stop you.

CAULIFLOWER CRUST PIZZA

I don't know, man, sometimes I just want to eat a pizza, or as was the case last week, I am invited to a pizza party and need to rustle up something. This pizza was a little bit complicated. I mean it's not so tough that you need to block out a week to prepare, but there are steps. Also, this pizza is a veritable cheese bomb. There's cheese in the crust, there's cheese on top, there's all the cheese you have to eat while you're grating the cheese. So if you're not eating dairy, move on, cover your eyes, and pray for us.

For the Crust:

Small head Cauliflower

3 eggs

1 cup mozzarella cheese

1 tablespoon dried oregano or Italian seasoning

salt and pepper to taste

Toppings:

can of pizza sauce

shredded mozzarella

sliced peppers

pepperoni

etc

The first step is ricing the cauliflower. I used a whole small head of cauliflower. Look, it was a week ago and I don't remember exactly how much. Put the florets in a blender or processor or use a knife (poor you) and make that cauliflower really small. Like smaller than rice grains actually, if you can remember what those look like.

We don't have a microwave because we're hippy conspiracy theorists, but if you did you could nuke the cauliflower rice. I used a pot and a lid on the stove, over medium heat, and I added a smidge of water. Cook until the cauliflower starts to soften and weep. And this part is weird but next wrap up the hot cauliflower in a towel or cheese cloth and twist and squeeze (careful baby it's hot) until its pretty dry and looks like dough. Crumbly dough.

Put this into a bowl with 3 eggs and a cup of grated mozzarella. (Use the dry stuff, not the suspended in brine stuff for this part, we want the crust to be dry.) then add a bit of oregano, maybe a tablespoon? And some salt? A pinch? Just some general Italian style seasonings. And mix it up with a spoon. Oh lord you can add so much to this.

Crap did I tell you to preheat your oven? 350F please. Go back in time and do that first.

Spread out some parchment paper on a baking sheet. Form some pizza crusts. Do not use your hands or try to spin it up in the air--that would be messy. I recommend making many smaller pizzas, since this doesn't have that much structural integrity. And bake until they start to brown a bit. And look firm. No, you don't need to look sternly at the pizza, I mean to make sure the eggyness looks cooked is all.

Now I made my own pizza sauce by using a can of tomato paste and some Italian spices and garlic powder and water and heat. You can do that or just buy some. But I think you should still heat it up.

If I need to tell you how to top a pizza I'm so sorry about your life. I hope it gets better. I used sauce, two or three types of cheese, Coppa salami, green bell peppers, and mushrooms sautéed with garlic and olive oil. Then I baked it again until it was hot and bubbly and brown. Then, agonizingly, we biked it over to the party in Chris's cargo bike. So it was a bit cold when we ate it but it was still delicious and all the vegans at the party loved it.

SIMPLE MEATZA

For the crust:

2 pounds assorted ground meat: sausage or chicken or hamburger or turkey (don't use only ground chicken though)

Garlic powder

Dried Oregano

Salt and Pepper

This is probably the easiest pizza recipe. It is so simple. You will like it.

Preheat oven to 450 degrees

You'll need a large cast iron skillet, or a rimmed baking sheet, because the meat will weep its juices into the pan, or onto the bottom of the oven.

Take some ground meat, it can be pork, or pork sausage, or chicken sausage, or beef, or a mixture of any of the above. I like to mix italian sausage and ground beef. If it's unseasoned meat, add some oregano and garlic powder and salt and pepper to it, and mix it up, and smooth it into the pan, all the way to the edges. The meat will shrink up as it cooks, so make it pretty thin. Cook for fifteen minutes, or until it's browned and cooked through.

Remove the crust from the oven and top with sauce, vegetables, cheese, and put back in for a few minutes to warm the toppings.

You're probably not going to want to eat this with your fingers, but you can, especially if you're under 5.

ZOODLES & SAUSAGE SAUCE

FOR THE ZOODLES:

Zucchini, about 1 per person

Salt

For the sauce:

1 pound of sweet Italian bulk pork sausage

1 package bacon

1 onion, diced

3 carrots julienned or thinly sliced

1-2 tablespoons Oregano or Italian Seasoning

5-8 cloves of garlic

1/4 cup red wine or stock

1 can tomato paste

1 bottle of strained tomatoes (16 ounces)

Salt and Pepper to Taste

Optional 1-2 cups baby spinach

First of all, you need to know how to make Zoodles, or zucchini noodles, whether you are going to be Paleo or not. Because Zoodles are a thing of beauty, and they are easy. Well, okay, they are a little bit annoying to make, and you need a special tool. You need a julienne peeler. And you need to accept that you will have little zucchini strings around your kitchen for days. And maybe some blood. But trust me, it's worth it.

Wash your zucchini and remove the stickers.

Then peel them with the julienne peeler into a colander. Peel until you see the seeds, then stop. Yes, it feels wasteful. Alternatively, you can slice them into linguine sized noodles, which is maybe less fun, but still delicious. Also, you use the whole zucchini, so it is less wasteful.

Now, use some sea salt, maybe one or two teaspoons—I never measure—and mix it up in the noodles. Just coat them so that all the noodles have a bit of salt. Not a ton. And wait. Put a bowl under the colander to catch the water that'll drain off the noodles. Wait at least 20 minutes, up to an hour; the longer you wait the firmer the noodles will be.

Now I'm not a scientist, and I'm lazy, so sometimes I squeeze the noodles to remove excess water, and sometimes I don't. But I know that you MUST RINSE the noodles unless you like salt noodles. Trust me. Salt noodles will ruin your day and you'll be up all night drinking water and peeing.

As for the sauce, brown some sausage and bacon in a big pot, then remove the meat but leave about a tablespoon of the grease. Then add one chopped onion and some julienned carrots until the onions are starting to brown. Add spices like oregano or Italian seasoning. Then add chopped garlic and stir for a minute. Add a bit of wine and tomato paste. Then add the strained tomatoes. Put the meat back in, and some chopped spinach. Cook on medium for a while. The longer the better. Serve over zoodles. Boom. Dinner.

STEAKTIPS AND TRICKS

There's, like, one million different types of steak. Some are pretty cheap, some are very expensive. You know that.

If you buy some expensive steak (rib eye, filet), if you're lucky and feeling meaty, please don't do much to it. Rub it with salt and pepper, and let it sit out at room temperature for a while. Up to an hour.

Then get your cast iron pan super hot. And sear that steak on one side. Maybe three minutes? Then flip it over and turn the heat to medium. Three minutes. Then flip it over again, and add a pat of butter to the top and watch it slide and melt and sizzle. Flip again, add butter, and use a thermometer to see how cooked it is. You really should have an instant read digital thermometer if you are going to be cooking meat, as this is the most accurate way to determine doneness without cutting into it.

Rest your meat (hahahah) on a cutting board and put a little aluminum blanket over it. Pour some wine into the pan and scrape. Or you can use another liquid (broth is great). OR, and this is amazing, put some steamed kale or some cooked mushrooms in and stir them around to soak up all of that yummy steak stuff. Boom. Best steak ever.

If you buy a cheaper cut, like a flank steak or hanger steak or London Broil, then you should marinate it in the fridge. I use Tamari or Coconut Aminos, some acid (usually apple cider vinegar), some oil (olive or sesame), mustard, honey, and black pepper. I still recommend taking it out of the fridge for a little while before you cook it, unless you want a really raw steak. I like my steak medium-rare. But I'm happier if it's more on the medium side.

The reason I like to let my steak warm up before I cook it is that I cook using a high heat method (I like the crunch), and if I start with the steak too cold it ends up burning before it's cooked. The reason I like to let it rest is so that it stays juicy!

Stay Juicy,

<3 Amy

LAMBHAM BURGERS

Mix equal parts ground lamb and ground beef with some dried oregano (or greek seasoning), and salt and pepper. Make into patties and grill or fry over medium high heat. Serve with lettuce wraps, or sliced up pepper buns. Delicious!

SIDE HUSTLES

Eat a variety of vegetables. (Did you just fall asleep reading that sentence? I know I fell asleep writing it. It's like, GOD MOM I KNOW I should eat lots of different colors and types of vegetables, and I should eat some raw and some cooked. Stop treating me like a child.) You'll be getting the bulk of your calories from meat and fat, but the bulk of your plate should be vegetables.

The simplest preparations, where the flavor of the vegetable gets a chance to shine, are often the best. I'm not going to give you a ton of vegetable recipes, because honestly I mostly cook the same things over and over again. But if you want to, there are so many great cookbooks just dedicated to vegetables, like *Chez Panisse Vegetables*, or anything by Debra Madison. And most of those recipes are already paleo friendly, or very easily adjusted.

ROASTING CAULIFLOWER/BROCCOLI/ CARROTS/GARLIC

This one time a long time ago we had some close friends over for dinner. And I was nervous and ambitious, as I tend to be, and got distracted by something elaborate I was making, and probably by all of the whiskey I was drinking, and left the cauliflower and broccoli in the oven for too long at too high of a heat.

Or so I thought. The florets came out of the oven, crispy, browned, almost to the edge of burnt, and caramelized. They were a hit.

But I forgot about them (maybe it was the whiskey?), until I read a recipe in _Salad Daze_ for basically what was my mistake. My method is more user friendly than the _Salad Daze_ one, but it does take longer.

Preheat your oven. You have some choices here. If you're roasting a chicken or otherwise using the oven, you can go with that temperature. But at least 400 degrees is where you'll want to start, and 500 degrees is the fastest, most living on the edge way to do it.

You can use a big cast iron skillet, if you have one big enough. Or a roasting pan.

Chop up your heads. With cauliflower, I like to slice the head in half, then remove the big stem and leaves, then pop the smaller florets out. It's fanciest if you get them all roughly the same size, but if your dinner guests are like mine and enjoy a variety of levels of done-ness in their vegetables, feel free to be wabi-sabi. For the carrots, if they are small and cute I like to just wash them and throw them in the pan, but if they are big and assertive I like to chop them into rounds. Cubes are nice too, as the corners tend to crisp better, but how much time do you have, really?

Now put your vegetables in the pan, and put the fat of your choice in there too. If it's butter or another saturated fat, make sure to stir everything after a few minutes in the oven to make sure nothing sticks.

Put the pan in the oven. Stir it up after five minutes, then periodically move everything around. It can take as long as an hour to get the caramelized results at 400 degrees Farenheit, and as little as 20 minutes at 500 degrees.

You might be tempted to add onions or garlic to this, and you can, but it's risky. Garlic tends to burn. Sometimes it doesn't though. Adding chopped garlic for the last couple of minutes works really well, though, if you can remember to do that.

Towards the end you can add the more fragile vegetables, such as haricots verts (skinny green beans).

ROASTED GARLIC

If you really want roasted garlic, here's what you should do: chop the top off of a head of garlic. Now examine the cloves and remove any that look moldy or dried up (I don't know what's wrong with me, but my garlic is always going moldy). Take a sheet of aluminum foil, put the garlic on it, pour a little olive oil or coconut oil on the top, twist the foil up around the garlic, sealing it up, and put in a 400 degree oven (or 350 or 375) and take out after 45 minutes or whenever it feels soft and squishy. Wait a minute before you eat though because that sucker is hot.

CUCUMBER AND TOMATO SALAD

This salad is almost a Greek Salad, in fact, if you feel like adding some feta cheese, please do. Irma and I got really excited about this.

To make the dressing, whisk together in a bowl:

2 tbsp Apple Cider Vinegar

3 tbsp Olive Oil

2 tsp (or more) Dried Oregano

(Optional garlic powder, just a sprinkle)

salt and pepper to taste

Add to this:

One peeled and chopped cucumber

One cup sliced cherry tomatoes (or other kind)

FRIED PLANTAINS

1 plantain per person, the darker ones are sweetest

Generous amounts of coconut oil or ghee suitable for high heat

Salt

I got really into plantains and pupusas when I was pregnant the first time, mainly because we lived close to the best pupusaria in the SF Bay Area. Or at least they said they were the best.

There is a trick to fried plantains. The plantains need to be very ripe, almost entirely black, if you want them to be sweet. Peeling is tricky too. You can slice the peel lengthwise, then carefully slip your finger between the peel and the flesh. Then you can slice the plantain.

In a pan over medium heat, add a generous amount of oil. Ghee is good, and coconut oil is really good. Add sliced plantains, sprinkle a bit of salt, and cook until browned on the first side. Move them around gently as they cook so that they don't stick. Then flip, and brown.

KALE IS SUCH A HIPSTER

My daughter is floating in a tepid bubble bath asking me to be the "Angry Queen" right now so that she can be Snow White, and then she wants to know if I'm going to kill her. And if I say "no I'm not going to kill you" she gets upset, so I end up saying "I'm gonna kill you Snow White!" Over and over until she leaves me alone.

Anyway, kale. It's probably good to eat it and it shouldn't be too hard to cook it in an appetizing way. I'm going to tell you my old stand-by. It involves butter. Or olive oil or whatever fat you're into.

1 bunch of kale, any kind, even collards, actually any of the tougher leafy green vegetables will work here, like mustard greens or bok choi

1-2 tablespoons of olive oil or butter or coconut oil

optional: red pepper flakes, chopped garlic, splash of white balsamic vinegar, squeeze of lemon

Take your kale and rinse it. It might be sandy and dirty so rinse it. Then stack the leaves up and slice it thinly perpendicularly to the center stem. Compost the bottoms. Then slice perpendicular to the first cuts so that the kale pieces are smallish. Then rinse the small itty bitty parts but don't dry them off.

In a large pot put two tablespoons of fat and the dripping wet kale pieces. Turn the heat to low and cover. In a few minutes stir the kale so the stuff on top gets to the bottom, you know like how people stir things up. Put the cover back on. Stir occasionally until the kale is wilted and about half as voluminous. Then turn off the heat and either serve right away, or, if you're like me and like your vegetables overcooked, cover and let steam in the remaining heat until whatever else you're having is cooked. Season with salt and pepper and maybe some more butter, why not? Maybe a splash of white balsamic vinegar or a squeeze of lemon?

Look, there is so much more you can do with kale, or even with this recipe, like you could sauté some garlic in the oil for a bit before you add the kale. Or red pepper flakes. The thing is, it's not hard and you can do it. Yes, sometimes I burn the kale because I'm in a hurry and try to cook it faster, but it's not like this takes a lot of time. The washing and cutting is the hardest part but it goes much faster with a glass of organic hippy no detectable sulfites wine. You deserve that wine, look at how healthy your dinner is! You're cooking KALE.

MARINATED KALE SALAD

1 bunch of kale (I love the curly purple kind for this)

Olive oil

Apple cider vinegar

Salt and pepper to taste

Is this even really a recipe? Wash and slice up some kale, removing the thickest part of the stems. Chop it up pretty finely. Put it in a salad bowl. Add olive oil and apple cider vinegar and salt and pepper. To taste. Chris's Aunt Francine makes the best salads and she doesn't ever measure, she tastes as she goes. So I started doing that too.

Think about massaging the kale. That's what it is. A kale massage. And if you're anything like me, it's a messy massage. Put it in the fridge in a sealed container. It'll keep for days, only getting better.

NO, YOU'RE THE SWEET POTATO

Sweet Potatoes are just amazing and delicious. Try all the kinds, the garnet yams, and the Japanese ones. I like to bake a lot of them all at once because they don't take up a lot of space in the oven, and they are good cold.

Sweet potatoes, or garnet yams, or jewel yams, or Japanese sweet potatoes

Butter or coconut oil for serving

Wash them, put them in a 400 degree F oven for about an hour, or until they are soft. Maybe line the bottom of your oven with aluminum foil first, or roast them on a tray, as they tend to caramelize and leak and it's a pain to clean. Not that I ever clean my oven, at least not until I'm about to move. Then I clean it.

You can put the ones you don't eat in the fridge. Then you can scoop out the yummy cooked flesh and use it to make a cake or pancakes. Or you can slice them up and pan fry the circles in butter. Or you can eat them cold and pretend they are ice cream cones.

Now for lunch boxes, or just when I feel awesome, I'll cube the potato and toss the cubes with olive oil and salt and pepper (or even some curry powder if I'm feeling extra awesome) and roast on aluminum foil or parchment paper covered baking sheets at 400 degrees, turning every ten minutes, until crispy and done. Smaller cubes get crunchier and cook faster. You can also use butternut squash for this.

You can also slice them into chips and make chips, but I always burn those so I stopped.

SOAK YOUR NUTS

Years ago I heard about a book called *Nourishing Traditions* by Sally Fallon. It's a good book. It's got some great stuff in it, and some stuff I don't agree with, and that's fine! We don't always have to agree. One of the things I learned from this book is how to soak and dehydrate nuts. The fancy word for this process is sprouting. When you sprout your nuts, you're tricking them into thinking they are going to make it. See, nuts and seeds and grains all want to make more nuts and seeds and grains, so they have protective enzymes that keep them from sprouting until the conditions are right. These enzymes also inhibit digestion. Which means, loosely, that we don't get all of the beneficial nutrients out of nuts. When you sprout nuts, you are getting them to start the germination process, and that makes them even more nutritious.

It sounds like maybe you probably don't need to go through all the trouble, since nuts are usually delicious just as they are. Except. Except when you try these nuts. These. Nuts. Are. Delicious. They don't make your stomach hurt if you eat a lot of them, like regular, unsprouted nuts can.

Raw nuts

Sea Salt

Time

I'm not going to give you exact measurements for this, since I never measure and it always turns out just fine.

Buy some raw nuts from the bulk section (organic if you can swing it). I've found this works best with Almonds, Walnuts, Pecans, and Hazelnuts. Cashews are not ever really raw, but you can soak them for six hours.

Go home.

In a large bowl put about a tablespoon of sea salt. Add some filtered water to dissolve the salt. Add the nuts. Cover with water, and stir. You want about an inch or two of water over the top of the nuts, as the nuts will absorb the water.

Cover the bowl (I usually use a dinner plate) and let soak overnight. 12 hours.

Drain the nuts and rinse in a colander.

In a warm oven (less than 150 degrees) or a dehydrator, spread out the nuts on a (lined) baking sheet and let dehydrate for a day. I often salt them too. Not always. I taste them as they dehydrate and take them out when they are dry.

If you want to, you can crank the oven up to 350 for the last fifteen minutes of cooking for an extra roasted flavor.

PALEO BREAD

In between discussing cannibalism, why we can't marry each other, and our inevitable mortality with my almost 3 year old, I made this loaf. Here's the recipe:

2 cups soaked and dehydrated almonds or other nuts

1/2 tsp baking soda

1/4 tsp salt

1/8 cup flax seeds

1/8 cup sesame seeds plus additional to top, optional

2 tbsp coconut flour

1/4 cup cashew and coconut oil blend (homemade) or store bought coconut butter or other nut butter

1 tbsp Apple Cider Vinegar

4 eggs

1) Preheat your oven to 350 degrees. In food processor type thing, blend the almonds until they are almost a flour. This part is annoying and takes a lot of work. Sorry. You could buy almond meal/flour, but I can't handle eating it in great quantities, so soaking and dehydrating the almonds beforehand makes this bread easier on my belly.

2) Add the baking soda, salt, flax seeds, sesame seeds and coconut flour and mix.

3) Add the remaining ingredients and mix until it turns into a dough. A wet dough.

4) Grease a small loaf pan (I used pastured butter) and pour batter into pan. Put in the oven. Bake for 30-40 minutes. It should puff up a lot and brown.

About the cashew/coconut oil blend: I made my own cashew butter but it doesn't get smooth unless I add oil. I am not sure about the proportions, but I'd guess it's about 75% cashew. To make this, just put 3 parts nuts and one part coconut oil in a food processor and blend until smooth.

DESSERT

Is it dessert that puts the sparkly glitter in a paleo unicorn's mane? No, that's magic. But dessert is pretty great, especially at celebrations.

I could tell you to eat dessert rarely, but you don't need to hear that from me. What you do need to hear is that it's okay to celebrate with food! That's a lot of what culture and community are all about.

It's a bummer to go to a party and not be able to eat anything there, so I started making my own things and bringing them to share, because that's a good way to make new friends. Or maybe it's creepy to stand by the food and tell everyone to try the thing you brought, and watch them until they do?

There's lots of things you can eat for dessert, and they don't have to be sugary or complicated to feel good. A bowl of fresh berries and a square or two of really dark chocolate is good for you, and delicious! Part of transitioning over to a healthier way of eating is shifting your body's perception of sweetness. I get to the point occasionally where I feel like carrots are really sweet. I am not suggesting you serve carrots for dessert at a dinner party, though.

BANANA ICE CREAM

1 frozen banana per person

optional: 1 tsp nut butter per person (cashew butter is luxurious for this)

optional: splash of vanilla, tsp of cocoa powder, chocolate chips, etc

If you have banana starting to go mushy and brown, peel them, line a pan that'll fit in your freezer with parchment paper, and break up the bananas onto the paper and freeze them until solid, then put them into an airtight container in the freezer until it's really hot, too hot to go buy ice cream. Then blend the ingredients together until mushy. A food processor works great if you're doing more than two bananas at a time. The nut butter is optional, but I love it.

FROZEN CHOCOLATE BANANA NUT BALLS

1 cup sprouted and dehydrated almonds and cashews (you can use non soaked nuts too)

1/4 plus 1/8 cup raw cacao powder

1 cup shredded coconut

1/4 cup coconut oil

2 tsp vanilla extract

1 banana

It's getting hot in here, so let's make some nut balls! I am getting so hot, I'm going to make some nut balls.

I made a version of these when Cary and Meri came over for dinner, but this recipe is more elegant, smoother, less sweet. You can always add some honey or maple syrup to these. Taste as you go, that's what I do.

So what I did was put the nuts and coconut in my ninja blender with the cacao powder and blended for a while until it was pretty smooth. Then I added the coconut oil and vanilla and blended again until it was almost the texture of nut butter. Then I added the banana and blended until that was, well, blended. Taste for sweetness. You might want to add some honey if you want a sweet treat.

Then I lined a plate with parchment paper and scooped out balls using my mini ice cream slash cookie scooper. Make them not too big is my advice, since they really take a while to eat. Then I popped that plate into the freezer until they were good and frozen. Then I ate a bunch. Yum!

FRUIT CRUMBLE

Once in a while I get on a pie kick. I found this pretty good coconut flour pie crust recipe, and I made pies, all kinds of pie with it, and it was good, except the first time I made the recipe it was amazing, and then every time after that it was not as good. But I kept trying to recreate that heavenly first crust, and so we ate a lot of pie, except that I ate most of the pie because, pie. Eventually I gave up because I realized I was chasing a memory of a fleeting moment of flaky perfection.

Crumbles, however, are easier than pie (see what I did there?) and you don't even need the crumble part. YOU CAN JUST BAKE SLICED APPLES AND CINNAMON and some butter and a pinch of salt and it will be pretty damn delicious. You can eat it with yogurt for breakfast. You can eat it warm out of the oven or cold out of the fridge. You can pack it in a lunch box. You can cook it until it is applesauce or take it out while the apples are still crisp. My grandmother used to put whole, cored apples in a baking dish with some cinnamon and raisins and butter and just bake them in a dish.

Here is my general crumble topping method. You probably need a food processor for this, but elbow grease would work as well.

Take some nuts, a cup or so, and chop until they are pea sized. I like cashews and almonds the best, but pecans are great too. Add some butter or coconut oil (a quarter cup is a place to start) and cinnamon and process more. Optionally, add raisins or chopped dried apricots. You can also change the spices up with cardomom or ginger. Feeling sweet? Add some maple syrup or honey. Not too much though.

For the fruit part, slice up apples, or pears, or persimmon, or pit some cherries, or berries. You know, the types of things you might find in a pie. Stir in some cinnamon, arrange in a baking dish, and spread the crumble over the top. Bake at 325 degrees F until the fruit is the desired texture. If you feel the crumble is getting too toasty, cover it with foil. Let it cool, then eat it all.

For some reason, kids love this. Okay I know the reason and it is that it is delicious and kids like delicious things just like we do because kids are people too.

TARTE TARTIN

What is this recipe? Because I know Julia Child would probably disagree with me about the name. It's basically sauteed apples with a puffy yummy top. Maybe you have a better name for it?

Take 5 Pippin apples (or some other baking apple), peel and slice them, and cook them in butter in a cast iron skillet (12 inch) until soft, but still firm. Add some cinnamon and other baking type spices, like allspice, cardomom, cloves, ground ginger. I used a spice mix from Penzey's Spices called Baking Spice, but then I ran out of it.

Sift into a bowl:

¼ cup almond meal

¼ cup coconut flour

¼ tsp sea salt

¼ tsp baking powder

1 tbsp cinnamon

1 tbsp baking spice

Add to this mix with an immersion blender:

4 eggs

1 tbsp vanilla

1 tbsp maple syrup (optional)

"milk" of your choice to thin if necessary

Add some more butter to the apples. Pour the batter over the apples in the skillet, and bake at 350 degrees until puffy and brown.

BIRTHDAY BLUEBERRY MUFFINS

My daughter's school is nut-free. And her classroom is also coconut and mango free. We eat a lot of nuts and coconut stuff.

I had to come up with something to bring to her classroom for her third Birthday. She wanted blueberry bran muffins (she saw it on tv), but you know bran is basically gluten so I had to lie to her about that. You may recognize this recipe as EXACTLY the same as the Banana Pancakes recipe.

Blend:

2 bananas

6 eggs

1 tablespoon vanilla

2 teaspoons cinnamon

Line a mini muffin tin with paper liners (or you could try to butter/oil it really well, good luck with that) and have someone tiny add

3 frozen blueberries (Counting Practice!)

to each individual tin.

Pour batter into tin. Bake at 350 until puffed up and done. 15 minutes?

These are not edible until they have cooled completely. Refrigerate them once they've cooled. It can be a challenge to get them out of the liners. But they were a hit with the kids and the teachers.

BLUEBERRY BIRTHDAY CAKE WITH TWO CREAM CHEESE FROSTINGS

Our three and a half year old rules our life. She chose this cake for Chris' 34th birthday. Well, she wanted a Blueberry Cake, and Chris wanted chocolate cream cheese frosting.

I didn't have enough coconut flour to make the only Paleo recipe I could find. I had to make something up. This is one of those times where my invention came out way better than I expected.

But this recipe does take time, and forethought. As in, you need to get your cream cheese and butter to room temperature ahead of time.

In a small sauce pan, put

1 cup frozen BLUEBERRIES

cover with ¾ cup MAPLE SYRUP

Okay I don't measure this part. But make sure there's enough maple syrup to barely cover the blueberries.

Bring to a boil, turn to low, and simmer until the blueberries turn really mushy and soft. Maybe 15 minutes. Then remove from heat and let cool. If you're in a rush or just generally impatient, you can put the pot in an ice bath and stir. Then you can blend this mixture if you want to. I did, because if I don't use my immersion blender for everything I feel like I'm missing out. If you don't blend it, you could strain the berry skins out. Actually, just blend it.

In a medium bowl, sift

⅓ cup COCONUT FLOUR

⅔ cup ALMOND FLOUR

½ tsp BAKING SODA

In smallish bowl, beat

6 EGGS (I had more like 5.5 because I broke one and caught it before it hit the ground. My skills are great.)

2 tsp VANILLA EXTRACT

½ tsp APPLE CIDER VINEGAR

Add the egg mixture to the dry mixture. Then add

1 cup of the berry maple syrup (reserve the rest for frosting)

Stir really well.

Butter and line a 6 inch round cake pan with parchment paper. Lots of grease. You could also do something else like cupcakes but this is what I did.

Bake at 350 degrees F for about 40 minutes, until the cake is set, and a toothpick comes out clean from the middle.

Let cool.

BEST FROSTING EVER

Frosting usually grosses me out. I mean, sure, when I was a teenager I would eat it straight from the can, no problem.

But let me tell you about a frosting that will amaze you in its simplicity and deliciousness. It takes a tiny smidge of planning. The planning is just that the ingredients blend best if they are all at room temperature. You can take them out of the fridge while the cake is baking and they will be softened by the time the cake is cooled. Unless it's really cold in your house.

Here it is.

Blend (I use my immersion blender in the smallest container the ingredients will fit in)

2 parts room temperature Butter (or coconut oil)

2 parts room temperature Nut Butter

1 part room temperature Maple Syrup or Honey (more or less, to taste)

Dash of vanilla extract

Pinch of salt (if there is no salt in the nut butter or butter butter)

Spread on your cooled cake while soft. If you put it in the fridge for a while, it hardens and is really super yummy.

BLUEBERRY CREAM CHEESE AND ALSO CHOCOLATE FROSTING

This frosting pairing was an improvisation. I was planning on only making the chocolate kind, but the bright purple changed my mind.

Everything needs to be at room temperature or a bit warmer for this to work.

In a mixer, put

8 oz CREAM CHEESE (this is the standard pack size)

8 tbsp UNSALTED BUTTER

Mix until smooth. You'll most likely have to scrape down the sides of the bowl if you use a stand mixer.

Add:

¾ cup BLUEBERRY MAPLE PUREE (or however much is left)

Continue mixing and scraping down the sides until the mixture is smooth.

Remove about half of the frosting and set it aside.

Add to the remaining frosting

⅛ cup COCOA POWDER

Mix. Keep mixing and scraping and tasting, adding ⅛ cup of cocoa powder at a time until the frosting tastes delicious. It gets quite stiff if you add a lot. I ended up with about a half cup cocoa powder total.

To assemble the cake, slice the cake into two layers using a serrated knife. Spread the chocolate frosting in the middle, put the top on, and spread the blueberry frosting on the top.

Eat immediately, or refrigerate and serve up to one day later.

IRMA'S SECOND BIRTHDAY CAKE

This is an actual recipe recipe, as in, I wrote it down and I follow it and the results are consistently amazing. I'm usually more loosey-goosey about cooking, but Birthday Cake is important to me.

Preheat your oven to 350 degrees F

Prep your pans. This is enough for one mini muffin tin and one 6 inch round cake pan. Line the muffin tin with paper liners, and oil the cake tin, line the bottom with parchment paper, oil the parchment paper, then sift cocoa powder into the tin to dust it.

Sift together in a small bowl:

1 cup cocoa powder

1 tsp baking powder

¼ tsp salt

In a larger bowl, immersion blend:

8 eggs

⅓ cup cashew butter

⅔ cup almond butter (or a mix of whatever nut butters you want equal to one cup)

1 tablespoon vanilla extract

⅓ cup coconut oil or butter

⅓ cup honey

Add the sifted cocoa powder mix to the bigger bowl and immersion blend until smooth.

Bake until puffed up and cracked. The mini muffins cook really quickly, twelve minutes or so, but the cake takes a lot longer. I use the mini muffins because they cook faster and I'm impatient, and also because I love tiny things.

Frost with Easiest Frosting Ever, or just spread some butter on those puppies.

EGG-FREE CHOCOLATE CHIP COOKIES

I adapted this recipe from Detoxinista.com, who I noticed had adapted it from somewhere else. It is very good.

Preheat the oven to 325 degrees Fahrenheit.

dry ingredients:

2 cups almond meal

1/4 teaspoon sea salt

1/2 teaspoon baking soda

wet ingredients:

1/4 cup butter or other fat, softened

3 Tablespoons pure maple syrup

2 teaspoons vanilla extract

1/2 cup dark chocolate chips, or a chopped up dark chocolate bar, the darker the better.

Mix the dry ingredients in a large bowl, then mix the wet ingredients into the dry ingredients, then add the chocolate. Scoop out the batter onto a parchment paper lined baking sheet, and bake for ten to twelve minutes until lightly browned.

EVEN MORE MAGICAL SUBSTANCES

What about Alcohol?

Well . . . I have some bad news and some good news. Bad news first: alcohol is toxic. It's not great for you, at least not in great quantities. The good news is that there have been some health benefits associated with low to moderate alcohol consumption.

So, if you want a drink and you don't have a drinking problem, I mean other than spilling a lot, which I do, go ahead! Instead of asking if a certain type of drink is paleo or not, when you drink you should drink drinks that are lower in sugar, and higher in beneficial nutrients, and also, since we're avoiding gluten, gluten free. Red wine, for instance, is usually low in sugar and high in anti-oxidants. I like tequila a lot, so I drink tequila and soda with a lime or orange wedge. I've heard this referred to as a Paleo Margarita. Let me be clear about one thing here: this drink tastes nothing like a margarita, it tastes like tequila, and if you don't like tequila a lot you will think it is gross.

CONCLUSION

Perfect Feminist Diet Plan:

Monday: Eat the Patriarchy

Tuesday-Sunday: Eat whatever is best for you.

As my grandmother Ann Lake Subach used to say, "Great minds run in the same ditch." She also used to say, "Everyone to their own taste, the old lady said as she kissed her cow." I had no idea what she meant back when I was a kid, but she repeated the same things over and over again, laughing at herself, so they stuck.

What I think she meant to pass on to me, now that I'm a grown up and she's been dead for sixteen years and can't tell me differently, is that there is value in following your own instincts and tastes.

It is difficult to do what makes you feel good, especially if it seems unusual to those around you. It can be alienating to go out for pizza with your friends and order a salad with no croutons and extra salami. But if you know that you're going to feel better eating salad than you would if you ate pizza, then you should eat the salad.

Here's the other thing: sometimes you want the pizza. And if you aren't celiac or wheat intolerant, if cheese doesn't bug you, or the place makes gluten free pizza, then get a damn pizza sometimes!

There's a lot of talk about the 80/20 rule in paleo circles.The idea is that you eat strictly paleo food (whatever that means) 80 percent of the time, and the rest of the time you give yourself a break. This rule, let's call it a guideline,

is what allows me to feel great, and also to have tacos and margaritas and whatever else I know is alright for me once in a while (I still cannot have gluten, sadly, but I'm mostly used to it).

If you view the world through a lens of deprivation—I can't have this, I can't have that, that's not paleo—you will feel deprived. If you view the world through a lens of abundance and self-care and self-nurturing—I'm choosing healthy food that will make me feel better instead of worse after eating it, I'm going to take a nap instead of working an extra hour—you will feel abundant and healthy and well!

Here's an old story about two kids, one an optimist, one a pessimist. They're both put in a room full of glittery unicorn poop. One of them says, "This is disgusting, how could you do this to me?" The other one of them says, "Yeah! There must be a unicorn in here somewhere!"

Okay, sure, sometimes you're stuck in a room of unicorn shit and there's no unicorn and it is disgusting. Sometimes life really does suck, and the world is full of one million unimaginable horrors. And it's hard to not get overwhelmed with a sense of despair or powerlessness. (I'm really bumming myself out here.) But there are still one billion little beautiful moments floating around, so maybe we could focus on the positive a little more, and take care of ourselves and each other in the face of the struggles and despair, and if all else fails there are some pretty good cat videos on YouTube, and you can always put on "Billie Jean" and dance around the living room.

Remember: you are a beautiful magical unicorn, and I love you.

RESOURCES

BOOKS:

Nourishing Traditions by Sally Fallon. There's a lot of gluten in this book, but also some great, traditional recipes. The author had a kind of hilarious feud with the paleo community, but I think they made up.

Chez Panisse Vegetables Tons of simple and unusual recipes, plus beautiful illustrations.

Salad Daze A mostly vegan book, with some gluten, but also they talk about awesome cheese. If you're looking to do some more complicated vegetable recipes, this is the book for you.

21-Day Sugar Detox A plan for getting off the sugar horse. I've never done the detox, honestly, but the book is pretty good. She offers different levels of the detox for people who need more carbohydrates or have special dietary needs.

Practical Paleo This is my favorite paleo cookbook. It is packed with charts and information and shopping lists and meal plans. It's also pretty accessible, with beautiful pictures and simple recipes.

Expecting Better by Emily Oster. I went to high school with the author, which is how I heard about this book. Emily is a brilliant economist who applied her critical thinking and research skills to all the shit our society tells pregnant women (and women who could potentially get pregnant), and examined the studies and figured out which advice was bogus (completely avoiding sushi for instance) and which advice was rock solid (tobacco is bad for fetuses). She lays out her findings and tells you what she decided to do (not everything is black and white) and trusts that women are capable of making the best decisions for themselves! What a radical idea!

Real Food for Mother and Baby: The Fertility Diet, Eating for Two, and Baby's First Foods, by Nina Plank. Filled with sensible advice on how to eat while pregnant, and how to feed the babe once it arrives, this book calmed a lot of my anxieties around babies and food. The author advocates baby-led

weaning, which means two things: extended breast feeding and offering the child the same foods that you're eating. The old science around feeding babies was extreme caution in introducing new foods one at a time on a strict schedule to avoid food allergies. It turned out that this might actually have been causing more food allergies, and that it's better to get those little immune systems exposed to all sorts of things early on.

PODCASTS:

Revolution Health Radio, by Chris Kresser

Balanced Bites

WEBSITES:

chriskresser.com

detoxinista.com

paleomg.com

whole9life.com

make your
own magic

ABOUT THE AUTHOR

Amy Subach is really great at pretty much everything she does! In addition to her sharp-witted sense of humor and all-encompassing compassion, she can make all sorts of cool things out of food or fabric or paper or noises. Basically, she's like the Buddha mixed with Bjork mixed with Picasso.